This is a work of fiction. Similarities to real people, places, or events are entirely coincidental.

ALTERNATIVE LANDSCAPES

First edition. November 23, 2019.

Copyright © 2019 Paula Puddephatt.

ISBN: 978-0-244-23854-4

Written by Paula Puddephatt.

Colour, Clutter, and Alternative Landscapes

Her office is full of colour and clutter. The walls are pastel pink - curtains, emerald green. This is my third appointment, and I don't quite feel comfortable with either therapist or environment, but I'm okay.

"So, what happened in *that* relationship, Janine?"

When I tell her, she'll ask me how I feel about it, even if it's ridiculously obvious how I must "feel about it". She won't attempt to give me the elusive "answers", or any sort of advice. She wants me to give *myself* advice - unlock the answers for myself - hidden, as they are, somewhere within my own mind.

I still don't really know whether this is a total waste of time, but I've been through the waiting lists for waiting lists just to get to this point. It would be crazy to walk out now.

"With Steve?" I know she means Steve. That's who we were just discussing, after all. I'm playing for time. I do that sometimes.

"Yes."

She isn't a natural blonde, of course. She must be roughly ten years older than me, I would guess - about forty. Maybe a little older - hard to tell, in this light - and her make-up is immaculate, of course. She's glamorous - hate that word - something I've never been, and never will be. I don't usually wish I was - just sometimes.

Like with Steve. Maybe it would have helped with Steve.

Yeah, *right*.

"He went off with a forty-five year old blonde called Sammy." It's almost fun, doing it this way, making her work for the truth. Oh, didn't I mention that the forty-five year old blonde called Sammy was *Samuel*, not Samantha? Well, I guess you never asked...

I'm looking between two different landscapes. There are fields and sheep, in the one in the oak frame. Next to it, is the window, revealing a view of wheelie bins and concrete. The one from our bedsit window - Steve's and mine - was more like the latter view. But you would need to add certain details - such as a few discarded lager cans, for a start - just to make the scene authentic.

We might be back in my childhood soon, of course. Since what happened with Steve, and all of the others, relates to that, anyway - and so, we are bound to end up there somehow. Back to my mum's three bedroom semi, with my brother and two sisters, and the cats.

Like, I can't *wait*, right?

I might go to Costa Coffee, after this appointment. I know it's going to finish in precisely five minutes, because I've just noticed her glancing at the clock.

A Little Red Dress and Some Wine

The little red dress showed off Joanne's firm breasts, slender waistline, and long, lean legs to advantage - to the extent that even her boyfriend, Dave, couldn't fail to notice. Her long, chestnut hair was loose, instead of tied back, as she normally wore it.

"More wine, babe?" she asked, not waiting for an answer, before reaching for the bottle, ready to refill his glass.

He was quick to cover the glass with one hand, lightly touching her arm with the other. "I'd better not, Jo - thanks all the same. I've got to drive home later."

"You could always stay the night. You know that, Dave." She brushed a strand of hair out of her large blue eyes.

"Yes, I know." He found himself studying the pale green table cloth.

"But you aren't going to, are you?" said Joanne, looking even younger than her twenty years.

"It's been a nice evening. Let's not spoil it," he suggested, allowing his eyes to meet hers again.

"The divorce will be through soon, won't it?"

Dave took a deep breath. He must remain calm. There was nothing to be gained by losing his temper with Jo - a fact learned through bitter experience. "Yes, I suppose it will."

"Do you think things will be better between us, once everything's - you know, sorted?"

"There's nothing wrong between us. At least, there wouldn't be, if you could refrain from nagging me for five minutes. I might as well still be married, when I've got you, moaning the whole time."

So much for staying calm. She did this to him every time.

Joanne got to her feet. "I'll clear the plates away - and the glasses too, if you won't have more wine."

"I'd love a coffee," he said, mainly to pacify her, but also because it was true. And Jo made great coffee - not like that instant muck he used at home.

Joanne nodded. "I'll make some coffee then, shall I?" She was talking very fast. "We'll have that, and then you can go home, and I promise I won't nag you any more. Did you decide what you're doing for your thirtieth?"

"Probably wondering what I'm doing, going out with a girl who hasn't even got her *twenty-first* to worry about for another ten months," he said, only half in jest.

"You're obsessed with my age." Matching Dave's light-hearted tone. And with the same underlying implication that her words were more serious than her playfulness might suggest.

Dave knew, in his heart, that he had been wrong to continue seeing Joanne for so long, when there was still a strong possibility that he and Yvonne would get back together - especially after last night.

He felt aroused just *thinking about* last night.

He had to tell Joanne the truth, of course. He knew that. But right then, the temptation was to stay the night, after all.

One last night of passion, before devoting himself to his wife and three kids. What harm could that possibly do?

The Boss

Stacey's eyes were unusual: wide-set and indigo. Her dark hair was shoulder-length, and shone with vitality, as if she had walked straight out of some shampoo ad. Today, she wore a red T-shirt, along with her navy-blue, fitted trouser suit. She was tall and slim, without being *too* slim - had "curves in all the right places", as they used to say.

Not that Frank was so out of touch as to tell Stacey as much, and expect his observation to be taken as a compliment. Nowadays, young women all aspired to be thin, with no stomach, and hardly any breasts - or, else, those awful implants, which didn't look in the least bit natural.

Steady on, Frank. Shouldn't even be thinking about Stacey's figure, and certainly not her breasts. She's young enough to be your daughter - and also happens to be your boss. The latter fact was almost unbelievable to Frank, who had, for over twenty-one years, run his own business. Now, he wasn't much more than a glorified filing and data entry clerk.

"Listen, Mark - I'll ring you back tonight, okay?" Stacey was saying. "I'm snowed under here, and really don't have time for this right now." She replaced the receiver, seeming uncharacteristically flustered. "Yes, Frank?" Her tone was polite, as always, but Frank detected a degree of irritation that was unusual for his, normally easygoing, line manager.

He handed her the document he had been holding, aware that his palms were on the sweaty side. Damn office heating.

"I came across this, in one of the files, and thought I should check it out with you. It seems that Mr. Baker..."

As Frank relayed the minor work-related query, Stacey visibly relaxed. Back into efficient business woman mode. She answered him clearly and concisely, with the standard, textbook response to this, obviously run-of-the-mill question, which newer staff members must have asked her countless times.

Frank was left to wonder about Mark, and the little girl, with long, blonde hair in bunches, whose photograph was blue-tacked to Stacey's PC.

"That's my daughter, Jessica," said Stacey.

The sudden change of subject took Frank by surprise. His turn to feel flustered. "I'm sorry. I didn't mean to...She's very pretty."

Stacey smiled. "I won't tell her you said so. She's vain enough, as it is. Jess *is* pretty, though. Doesn't look a bit like me, does she? The spit of her dad."

Frank didn't want to *think about* Jessica's dad. "You don't look old enough to have a daughter of - she must be at least eight or nine, mustn't she?"

"Nearly ten. I don't suppose I *am* old enough to have a ten-year-old, really. I was fifteen, you see, when Jessica was born."

Frank didn't know what to say.

"You don't approve, do you?" For a moment there, Stacey actually looked as if it bothered her, one way or the other, whether Frank approved of her or not. Vulnerability made her look even younger - and even sexier.

He imagined himself asking her: "Do you fancy a drink after work, Stace?"

Stace. That was what her younger colleagues called her. He longed to call her Stace, and run his fingers through her dark hair, with the copper highlights.

"I don't disapprove, Stace-y," he replied, ironically feeling as awkward as a teenager.

Their eyes locked - just for a moment. Stacey looked away first. She shuffled some papers around on her desk. He was dismissed.

Later, when Frank was checking his emails, he found one from Stacey. It was entitled: "Sorry". He clicked on the envelope icon.

Didn't mean to be stroppy earlier. How about a drink after work? It's hard to talk here. Stace.

Frank had to read the message about six times, before he was able to believe that he had received such an email - never mind considering how to answer it.

***

Stacey was picking at the label on her bottle of Budweiser. It still surprised Frank that the younger generation preferred to drink straight from bottles and cans, invariably declining a glass when offered, as Stacey had just done.

Frank wished that the background music could either be turned off or, failing that, up. At this level, all he could distinguish was that relentless bass line, characteristic of almost all pop music, recorded since the 1980s.

"I can only be half an hour, tops," said Stacey. "I need to get back for Jessica."

"Of course - no problem, love." The "love" echoed in his brain, and he wished he could snatch the word back. Did it sound like a "love" he would have used for a wife? Or a daughter, perhaps? Either way, it was wrong - inappropriate.

"Do you have children, Frank?"

"No." He hesitated. "Janice never wanted them," he added, almost apologetically.

"Janice? Is she your wife?"

Frank was taken aback. Stacey seemed unsure as to whether or not he was *currently* married.

In which case, why was she...?

Why was she *what*? Flirting with him?

"Ex-wife," said Frank, forcing himself to look Stacey in the eye, as he spoke. In the dim light of the quiet pub, she looked even more beautiful than she did at work. "How about you, Stacey? Who's Mark? Is he Jessica's dad?" Sounded awful, that - as though Frank believe that she was, in some way, answerable to *him*. "You don't have to answer that," he added, hastily.

"No - no, it's fine. Mark, who I sometimes talk to on the phone, you mean?" This with a faint, half-smile.

"Yes."

"He's my brother. Always in some sort of trouble, is our Mark. Jessica's dad is called Peter. I haven't seen or spoken to him for the past four years. He's entitled to access to Jessica, but no longer chooses to exercise the right."

"Janice did have two sons, in the end, with her second husband, Steve. So maybe it was just me."

"Apparently, Jessica has a half-sister now. She might be interested in that one day. I wouldn't mind, if she was. It's hard for her, being an only child." Stacey glanced at her watch.

"Do you have to go?"

"I'm all right for another ten minutes or so."

So am I, thought Frank.

And, beyond that...?

Lego

My four-year-old twin daughters are fighting over a piece of yellow Lego. Rebecca "gobs" (as she would call it) into Kayleigh's white-blonde curls, which could as easily have been Becca's own - had she not insisted upon having her hair cut somewhat shorter than Kayleigh would have allowed in "like, a million years" - quote, unquote.

***

I gratefully gulp down gin, from a half-empty bottle, which someone evidently dumped here last night. Was it me? I can't honestly remember. The neat alcohol burns my throat, and puts me instantly back in touch with my bodily sensations. Now, I can actually feel the cold, hard concrete, beneath my somewhat bony hands and wrists, as I climb out of what, last night, constituted my "bed".

It's really a tunnel, in a kid's adventure playground. My ex-wife and I used to bring the girls here - shit, how many years ago now?

But I don't want to think about Claire or the twins. It's bad enough that I still get those bloody dreams, night after night.

The girls must be seventeen now, going on eighteen. I probably wouldn't recognise them, and they definitely wouldn't know me. I wouldn't *want* them to, in my current state.

The dawn chorus is telling me that it's time to get my arse out of this "bed", which reeks of stale urine. Probably mine, but who knows?

Or *cares*, for that matter?

For my part, I'm past caring about much.

I ought to be getting back "home".

I live - well, exist - in a one-room bedsit, just outside the centre of Reading. This is where, as a rule, I tend to sleep, but I had a bit too much to drink last night and...Yeah, well - you catch my drift.

The sky is tinged with Kayleigh's favourite shades of pink and peach, which Becca, naturally, hates - or did then. That sky reminds me of a watercolour painting by the girls' mother, which probably still hangs in the large, magnolia-walled entrance hall of Claire's mum and dad's, in Orpington.

I happen to know that her parents still reside in that poxy bungalow of theirs, which I always hated visiting. At least three out of six of Mrs. Green's, now ageing, Labradors are, likewise, still around.

I've asked myself the question so many times now. Too many. But how can I *not*?

It's nothing more than a hoarse scream, nowadays: "Why? Answer me that, God! Why?"

Over a piece of yellow Lego. Everything - all down the fucking plughole.

Well, okay - so I didn't split up with Claire just because of some sodding Lego.

But it was the catalyst. I'd taken Rebecca's "side" once too often, and pretty soon Claire and I were at each other's throats.

Well, we were always at one another's throats, so why was this so different?

It was "different" because, this time, she chucked me out of the family home.

And subsequently filed for divorce - something which, no doubt, made her parents and sisters crack open their bottles of economy so-called "champagne", the moment they heard. Fucking vultures, the lot of them.

Of course, the bitch and her "clan" made certain I'd never get to see Rebecca or Kayleigh again. The last I heard, Claire and the twins were living in Spain, with her new bloke. Some fat jerk - accountant, apparently. Well, bully for her.

It's funny, isn't it? We survived so many things, Claire and I: family deaths, and family feuds; Claire's continuing to vote Tory, after I'd switched my allegiances to the Lib Dems; my affair with Claire's friend, Judy; my affair with Judy's husband, Robert...

My spell inside - for my part in an armed robbery, in which Claire's brother, Keith, was killed. That should, by rights, have been the end.

But it wasn't. You know that expression about the straw and the camel's back? Yeah, well - the "straw", in this instance, was a piece of yellow Lego.

The Club

It was all over, in a matter of minutes. That's the ironic part.

There were three of us: my best mates, Catherine and Vanessa, and myself. We'd been going to the local youth club for a couple of years, at the time.

It was okay. I mean, there *were* trendier places to hang out, on a Friday night. But, when you're thirteen, and have the misfortune to *look* it...

Remember those Panda drinks? Coke or shandy - take your pick. Both were cheap, and somewhat nasty. That was what they served at what they termed "the bar", although it wasn't one, as far as I was concerned - not if you couldn't purchase a pint of Stella or a bottle of Bud there.

They did, however, sell barely edible "Pink Shrimps", which retailed at 2p each. Alternatively, there were "White Mice" - a totally inedible bargain, at 1p per "Mouse". Ideal for lobbing at the acne-covered twelve- to fifteen-year-old "hunks", whom my friends and I were *far* too shy to chat up, *as such*.

The Club held discos, once a month. The three of us would dutifully, and somewhat unconvincingly, prance around, pretending to be Madonna, whenever the DJ played her latest hits, such as "Like a Virgin", "Material Girl", and "Into the Groove". In retrospect, he didn't play much else.

Well, there were the slow songs, of course. As none of us had boyfriends, we'd sit those ones out. Along with the inevitable "Crazy For You", there were "Careless Whisper" and "Move Closer".

I don't think the DJ could have had a particularly large record collection. Probably worked for our local radio station, come to think of it, as the playlist was almost identical.

Cath's elder sister, Tracy, helped out at the club, on a voluntary basis. Vanessa was, of late, incapable of acting like a sane human being, in Tracy's presence. This was on account of her jealousy - of Tracy's, unquestionably gorgeous, fiance, Matt. Catherine fancied him, too. I was the only one who *didn't*.

I didn't even especially *like* the guy, although I couldn't have told you why.

Catherine was playing pinball, as per usual. That girl was seriously hooked. And I, for my part, was becoming *seriously* bored, watching her. She could at least have had the credibility to get addicted to Space Invaders.

"Fancy buying some White Mice to lob at you-know-who?" whispered Vanessa, self-consciously tugging at what there was of that blood-red, PVC miniskirt, which Cath and I had failed to talk her out of purchasing. The item of clothing in question had been drastically reduced in price, and not without reason.

"Don't you think he's a bit old for us, Vanessa?" I suggested, tentatively.

"He's not *old*, Leila. He's younger than Tracy."

I stifled a sigh. *Not this again.* Yeah, okay, so Matt was younger than Tracy. He was nineteen, and Cath's sister would be twenty-two next month. Not *underage* though, was he?

But try telling *that* to Vanessa!

"Maybe you ought to take up pinball, like Cath," I muttered. "It's a lot safer."

"Sorry?"

"Never mind! Hey, Nessa - wait up, can't you? You know I can't run in these heels!"

My friend and I were both out of breath, sweaty, and flustered, by the time we reached "the bar". We turned out our pockets, searching for change to squander on sweets we had no intention of eating. Not necessarily advisable, when you're existing on paper round wages, topped up by very minimal "pocket money", but there you go. Vanessa would probably have considered the "Mice" an investment.

Some "investment".

I've been over it so many times, over the years - what happened to me, that night. If only I'd realised then, what Vanessa's idol - Tracy's fiance - was really like.

We should have stayed together. That was what Mum and Dad were always banging on about, wasn't it?

And it was true.

I was the only one who *hadn't* had some stupid crush on Matt. I hadn't even fantasized about having him ping my bra, like the other boys did. The boys my own age - the ones I'd still enjoyed flirting with, back then, before I'd known what any of it was really all about.

***

"What's the matter with you, Leila?" demands my boyfriend, as I roll on to my side, away from him, in the bed in which Tom and I have been sleeping together for - shit, it must be five years now, mustn't it?

And it was over in a matter of minutes, what Matt did to me.

Who the hell did I think I was kidding?

The Collection

I collect weight slips. You know, those pieces of paper, churned out by the digital scales, in Boots and Superdrug. The ones that tell you your actual, and allegedly "ideal", body weights.

I've got hundreds, literally. I keep them in the old biscuit tins, which Mum lets me have "for storage" - although she, of course, has no idea what I *actually* "store" in them. I don't always wash the tins out properly, and will often come across crumbs, which I find strangely comforting, in an almost masochistic way.

We've a pair of scales in the bathroom, but I don't use them much, as they're not accurate enough, for my purposes. It's the ones in chemists, and the local sports' centre, that I'm addicted to.

I know. "Addiction" is a strong word, isn't it? But that's what it is. It's not that different, in many ways, to being hooked on the slot machines, in amusement arcades. It's a buzz. Every time I stand on those scales, I experience the familiar rush of anticipation, mixed up with panic.

A couple of years ago, when I clutched, in damp, shaky hands, the unopened envelope, containing my GCSE results - that's about the closest anything has come to...

No, I tell a lie. *That* wasn't the closest. The best example would have to be the time I showed up at my boyfriend, Danny's, twenty-first. The party I hadn't been supposed to know about.

The party at which I caught my "boyfriend", examining the state of my elder sister, Sophie's, tonsils.

I'm looking for my "seven stone three". That's my "record", to date. I've only got the one, even though I've got two "seven-fours", and thirty-four "seven-fives".

Try not to panic, girl. It has to be here somewhere.

"Laura, are you nearly ready?" yells my mother. "We need to be off soon!"

"Just coming, Mum!"

I examine my reflection, in the full-length mirror. Hair and make-up both passable, I assure myself. But do I look fat in this dress, or what?

Not sure what I'm dreading most about this wedding. The reception afterwards? All that phenomenally calorific food, and every single relative I barely knew I *had*, conspiring to ensure that I actually eat some of it?

A great aunt or two will probably follow me into the loo - just to make sure I don't...Yes, well. You get my drift. So, is that the worst part, then?

Or is it the bitter irony of watching my sister get married to the bloke, for whom I spent three entire years starving, puking, and stepping on scales?

Watching our Sophie, walking up the aisle, looking totally gorgeous, in her long, ivory, Size Sixteen wedding dress.